Marge in Charge

Marge in Charge

ISLA FISHER

Illustrated by Eglantine Ceulemans

HARPER

An Imprint of HarperCollins*Publishers*

Marge in Charge
 For information address HarperCollins Children's Books, a division of HarperCollins Publishers, 195 Broadway, New York, NY 10007.
www.harpercollinschildrens.com

ISBN 978-0-06-266218-7

17 18 19 20 21 CG/LSCH 10 9 8 7 6 5 4 3 2 1
First U.S. edition, 2017. Originally published by Piccadilly Press, UK, in 2016.

For Olive, Elula, and Monty.
My favorite small people on the planet
and the best editors a writer could wish for.
—I.F.

the Button Family

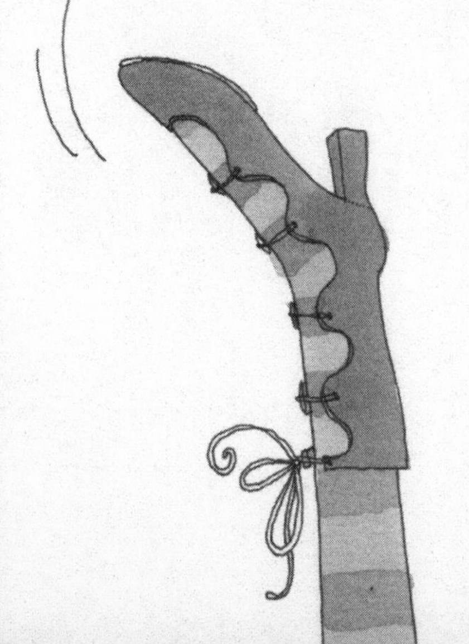

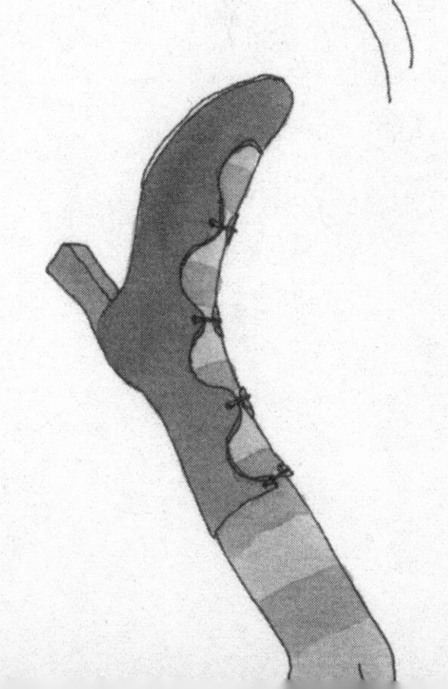

Marge Babysits

My name is Jemima Button. I am seven years old, and I'm the tallest girl in my class. My little brother is Jakeypants, though grown-ups call him Jake, and he is four years old. He loves wrestling, dinosaurs, and ice cream.

We live with our mommy and dad in an ordinary house, on an ordinary street. We used to be an ordinary family until the day our babysitter came.

It was five o'clock on a Thursday, and our family was sitting around the table. Our parents were dressed up in their fancy clothes.

"Why do we need a babysitter?" asks Jake.

"Because we are going out for dinner," explains Dad, patting Jakeypants on the head.

Mommy smiles and says, "We need someone here to look after you."

I can see that my baby brother is not happy. He begins to cry—well, fake cry. He wails and flails his arms around like a baby penguin on slippery ice.

"Do you want to read a story?" asks Dad, handing Jake his favorite book.

"Stupid book!" says Jake, and throws it on the ground.

Oh no. I bite my lip. When Jakeypants starts throwing things, it means he is headed for a tantrum. What will our new babysitter think? The last time we had a babysitter, Jake spent the whole time hiding in his room building a Lego weapon so that he could "destroy" her! He was mad at her because she scolded him for covering Dad's desk with stickers. And then *I* had to peel them all off!

I hope Jakey behaves himself tonight. He can be very stubborn and naughty when he wants to be.

"There's your favorite for dinner: macaroni and cheese," says Mommy as she puts it into the fridge.

Jake's face lights up, but not for long. ". . . and broccoli," he adds, scowling. "I don't want broccoli, and I definitely do NOT want a babysitter!" Jake shouts.

"Even if the broccoli is on your blue *T. rex* plate?" Mommy pleads.

"Especially then!" Jakey yells.

Mommy gives Dad a panicked look.

Everyone knows that my little brother has two rules:

1. He won't wash his hair—he says it's "boring."
2. He won't eat broccoli. Ever.

But then we meet someone extraordinary: our new babysitter.

DING DONG—that's the doorbell.

Jakey stops crying and races to the door. He peeks through the window then takes off his shorts and pulls them over his head. Jake always does this when he wants to wrestle or stop someone from coming into the house, like Uncle Desmond.

"Put your shorts back on," Mommy says sternly. Dad is opening the door.

"Meet Marge!" Dad says in the voice he saves for his boss at work.

I peep out from behind Dad since I always feel shy around new grown-ups.

There she is —
Marge, the babysitter!

Standing in our hallway is a person so small that she only comes up to Dad's armpit! She is wearing a yellow woolly hat and glasses. Her face looks serious too, and I worry that she will be strict, like my teacher

Mrs. Ratley, who made us eat all our bagged lunches even when the sandwiches were soggy.

She has a big, round belly and skinny legs with knees as knobby as twigs.

"Hi, Marge," I say, then give her my bravest smile.

But Jake has only noticed how small Marge is. She is definitely NOT tall enough to ride a roller coaster. She could even fit in Jake's cardboard box that he uses as his superhero hideout.

"Are you a kid or a grown-up?" he asks, peering closely at her. Marge thinks for a while.

"Ahh, definitely a grown-up," she answers finally.

"Then why are you so small?" demands Jake.

"Well, why are YOU so small?" asks Marge right back.

"Because I'm only four years old!" Jake rolls his eyes. He is excellent at eye rolling even though Mommy told him that it's rude to do it to grown-ups. "You look one hundred years old," he snorts.

Mommy and Dad look worried that Marge will be offended, but instead she throws her head back and laughs. This makes me feel a little bit less nervous, so I say, "I'm Jemima."

"Nice to meet you," Marge says solemnly, shaking my hand like adults do. It makes me giggle.

"Are you a Christmas elf?" asks Jake. "Let me see if your ears are pointy." Jake is now peering at the sides of Marge's head. Dad coughs nervously and steers Jake away from Marge. But I notice him glancing at

Marge's ears too.

"The rules are on the fridge," Mommy tells Marge. "If you have any questions, ask Jemima; she's my big girl. We will be back by eight o'clock." Then she turns to us. "Remember to be polite and say 'please' and 'thank you' when Marge takes care of you."

"We will," I promise.

I hear Mommy telling Marge that it's very important for Jake to eat all his dinner, especially the broccoli, and wondering if she could possibly try washing his hair? Then she gives Marge her cell-phone number for emergencies.

Mommy and Dad both give me a big hug. The butterflies in my belly aren't so fluttery now that we've met Marge. I am very curious about her but still nervous that my little brother might misbehave. To my surprise, though, he lets Mommy hug him good-bye, which he never normally does.

We stand on the doorstep on either side of Marge and wave as my parents leave. The minute the car is gone, we head inside.

"Are you a dwarf? From *Snow White*?" Jakey asks.

"No, and I'm not an Oompa-Loompa either," Marge says, laughing.

"Oompa-Loompas only exist in *Charlie and the Chocolate Factory*," I say.

"Are you a jockey? Do you gallop horses in a race?" Jake asks.

Marge shakes her head.

"Did you drive here? How did your little feet reach the pedals?" asks Jake.

"I am sure you can lower the steering wheel!" I offer helpfully.

"I actually use a booster chair," Marge says. Then she leans in secretively.

"Being small means I can visit the museum for half price!" she brags as she takes off her glasses and pea-green coat. Then Marge pulls off her hat. Guess what's underneath? Long, colorful hair that falls down her back! Green, blue, orange, red, and yellow hair like a waterfall of colors.

I wonder if Mommy would let Marge look after us if she saw her crazy hair!

"Wow!" I say.

Marge crosses her feet at the ankles and exhales. "I was born Margery Beauregard Victoria Ponterfois, and I am a duchess."

"A duchess?" I ask, blinking. "Are you Dutch?"

Marge laughs, and little creases form next to her blue eyes.

"No. The king of England's fourth son is my uncle Leonard."

"Do you have any children?" I ask.

Marge shakes her head. "But I have ten pets: three white miniature ponies, three swans, two polka-dot Pomeranian puppies, a long-tooth ferret, and an albino water buffalo."

I can barely breathe with excitement.

"I used to live at the palace, but the royal guards wouldn't allow my pets to sleep in my bed. Did you know that there are 779 rooms in the royal palace? I was always getting lost. Sometimes I would fall asleep looking for my bedroom! So my pet friends and I set out on an adventure to find a new home."

NORTH POLE: Alfie, Alvin, & Arnoldo the swans are not happy with new home: too cold.

Jakey is behaving really well, and I can tell that he's enjoying Marge's story.

"Have you ever been on a bus?" Jakey is obsessed with buses.

"Of course," Marge sniffs. "I have ridden a red double-decker bus, an airport bus, and a minibus . . ."

WOW! Jakey is really impressed now.

". . . but my favorite mode of transport is the royal coach pulled by eight palomino donkeys."

I want to ask Marge all sorts of questions about her animal friends and her life, but she jumps up and says, "Now, your mommy wants me to read the rules on the fridge. Hop to it!"

We follow her to the kitchen, and Marge reads the list aloud:

1. Dinner is at 5:30. There's macaroni and cheese and broccoli in the fridge.

2. Playtime next, but all toys must be put away afterward.

3. Bath time is at 6:30, and please try to wash Jake's hair.

4. Bed by 7:30.

I would much rather listen to more of Marge's story, but Marge is looking very serious now that she has read Mommy's list. "I think we might need to add a few new dinner rules," she says.

Jake groans, and my stomach sinks.

"I won't eat broccoli. Not now, not ever," says my brother stubbornly.

Marge just raises one eyebrow as she grabs a napkin and starts to fold it. "I have been to many exotic dinners

all around the world. I have dined with princesses, knights, lords, and ladies, and I have my own royal dinner-making rules," says Marge as she finishes crafting the napkin into a splendid chef's hat and pops it onto her own head.

Jake and I exchange an excited look. *Our new babysitter is going to let us cook!* I race to the bottom drawer and find our aprons.

"Right, let's see . . . ," says Chef Marge.

Rule One: prepare the food. "Jemima, you will be the chef's helper."

I have no idea what that is, but I begin gathering all the ingredients that Marge tells me to, and Marge informs Jakey that he will be the waiter.

"Do waiters get to wrestle?" Jake karate kicks the air.

"Yes. But first they have to ask the dinner-party guests what they want for dinner and write it down on this little pad." She hands a notebook and a silver pen to Jake.

"But I can't write any words yet—except for my name." Jake sighs.

"Don't worry," says Marge. "I read squiggles! I can even read the handwriting of all my pets—how else do you think we communicate?"

WOW! I have always wondered whether chickens could handwrite, or rather claw-write.

"It all started when my camel asked me to translate a love letter she had received from a dairy cow. Now that was tough, because cows don't use their hooves for writing. . . ."

"What do they use, then?" asks Jake.

"Their tails, of course!" cries Marge, giving Jakey and me a bowl. "You know, Prince Leonard won the heart of my aunt with a red velvet birthday cake. Baron Dinklestitch wasn't pleased, mind you. . . ." Marge takes three eggs and tries to juggle them. All three drop and smash onto the floor.

Jake and I crack eight new eggs into a bowl. Jakey scoops up the shells and yolks from the floor and throws them into the bowl too, and we just cover it all in a pile of flour. Then we add a mountain of cereal and a tea bag for good measure. Marge tells us she thinks that we are very creative chefs, but I am not sure Mommy would agree with that.

Once everything is cooking nicely, Marge gets the list out again and adds another new rule.

Rule Two: set the table.

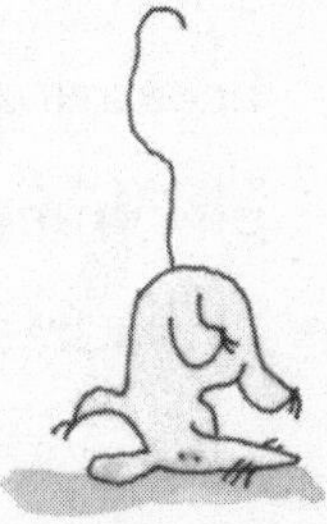

Jake groans. But Marge tells us it's the only way to decide on our guest list for the dinner party.

"You mean we're inviting guests to eat with us?" I ask.

"Of course!" she replies. "Dinner should always be a party, and the perfect number for a dinner party is six."

So we decide to include Archie, our pug-nosed puppy dog. But we still only have four!

"We will set the table for six anyway, and maybe some special guests will surprise us," Marge says.

We place three plates and three forks and knives for every guest. But because Archie can't use cutlery, I give him a pair of chopsticks.

"What's next on Mommy's list?"

I ask Marge, hoping she'll have some more extra rules.

Marge toots a pretend trumpet.

. . . *Rule Three: decorate the dining room!*

Soon we are cutting out cardboard stars and making streamers, and Jake staples the stars onto the tablecloth. Then he gets carried away and staples his T-shirt to his shorts and staples one of his socks to a dish cloth, and he is about to staple

Archie's tail to his leg when Marge swoops in.

"Can I borrow the stapler?" Marge asks, and hides it quickly.

Jake tapes Pete, his toy stegosaurus, to the center of the table as a decoration, and we tie a ribbon on the back of everyone's chair. I only just learned how to tie a bow, and I can do it quite quickly now.

"A room fit for kings and queens!" Marge says, and high-fives us both. "And perfect for a duchess. It's all ready for dinner now."

PHEW! My tummy is making funny grumbly sounds, and I can smell our cake baking in the kitchen, but then Marge checks the list again.

"It's time to get cleaned up so we can look fabulous for our dinner party," Marge says. "Bath time!"

Bath time before supper? This is very unusual, but Marge is in charge, so we follow her upstairs.

In the bathroom Jake refuses to run the bath or get his towel. I am worried because I know how stubborn my little brother can be, but Marge has a fun idea. She fills the sink with water all the way to the top and empties in a *whole* bottle of lavender bubble bath. It's

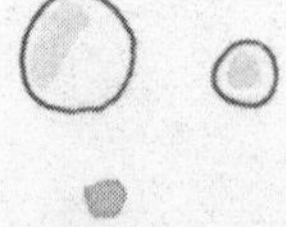

incredible—bubbles are floating serenely onto the floor and covering our toes.

Then she tips in a bottle of apple shampoo, Dad's aftershave, and Mommy's face cream, and she even sprays in some fancy perfume.

Jakey holds his nose "Phew-eee," he says, giggling.

Then Marge somehow finds our swimming goggles, which have been lost for ages, and we put them on. She also pulls out a whistle. "It's time to dunk!" she cries, blowing it hard. "One, two, three—

DUNK!"

Jakey and I plunge our heads in the sink and under the faucet, then up again. Soon we are surrounded by bubbles floating under our chins and around our ears! Jakey makes a Santa beard, and I make a white wig of foamy bubbles.

"Shall we wash the dog too?" Marge asks, and I can hear her spraying more air freshener around the room. I can't even see her anymore through all the bubbles.

"No," I say. Archie hates the water and will only go in the pond at the park if he's chasing a ball.

"But didn't the list say we need to wash Archie's fur?"

"No," I say, "Mommy wrote 'Jake's hair,' not 'Archie's fur'!"

I'm feeling nervous again—but this time it's not about Jakey misbehaving. I'm worried that we might not get through the things on Mommy's list on time, and also my eyes are full of soap.

Suddenly Marge pops her head through the bubbles and grins at us. "Do you want a shampoo Mohawk?"

Jake nods, although neither of us even knows what a Mohawk is! Marge lathers up Jake's hair with shampoo until it stands in one point on top of his head. He looks like a white rooster. Then she lathers up mine too, like an ice-cream-cone head.

As I wipe the soap out of my eyes, I can see that the bathroom is a bit of a mess, but Jake has clean hair and is happy, and Mommy will be so happy too!

"What's this shelf?" Marge asks. I can vaguely see through the white fluffy clouds of foam that she has found Mommy's "out-of-our-reach" shelf.

She unscrews a large jar of something sticky and brown and rubs it all over her face.

"This must be a mud mask, to tighten the pores of the skin," Marge assumes. But I can read the label, and it clearly says BROWN HAIR DYE.

Oh no! Marge has put hair dye all over her face. It's turning orange. . . . She really does look like an Oompa-Loompa now!

"Quick, Marge, wipe it off!" I shout. "That is not a face mask!"

I don't want Marge's face to be the same color as Mommy's hair!

WHOOPEE! Marge plunges her face into the water in the sink and is scrubbing her cheeks! Now bubbles and water are all over the floor.

Archie trots into the bathroom and starts barking at Marge.

"I am Marge the Miniature Mermaid!" gurgles Marge as she pops back up.

"I told you she wasn't a real grown-up," Jake whispers to me, looking around at the messy bathroom. I'm a little worried—we've still got lots to do, and we haven't been following the list in order!

"Come on, Marge," I say. "It's time to get back to Mommy's list."

I have to say, it isn't easy finding Marge in those bubbles. They're everywhere, rising all the way up to the ceiling.

"Gotcha!" I say, grabbing her foot, but when I lift it, it's a bottle of shampoo!

"I have her elbow!" Jakey shouts, and then holds up a bag of bath salts.

We both crack up laughing!

"Marge, is that you?" I say, pulling out a tub of body wash.

Finally I feel something moving and grab at her. She feels very hairy and furry, and as I pull her out, I realize I have Archie in my arms! How did Archie get into the sink?

"Boo!" shouts Marge through a curtain of foam, grinning from ear to ear.

Once we are dry, Marge has a new idea. "What shall we wear to dinner?" she asks us—as if we are in charge, not her.

"Anything but shorts!" shouts Jake, his hair now clean and dry. Jakey HATES

shorts. Even in summer.

"We can't wear ordinary clothes," says our babysitter. "Going to a dinner party is a regal affair, and we have to look our best."

I have an idea. "I'll be right back!" I say, and I run off to find our dressing-up box. When I get back, I find Marge and Jakey in Mommy and Dad's room.

Jake is standing right inside Mommy's closet, pulling out all her favorite clothes. Oh no! Mommy will not be happy if we make a mess, and I don't want to get in trouble. But it does look like fun. . . .

"You can borrow my fairy wings," I offer Marge. "And my ladybug Halloween costume will fit Jakey."

Marge shakes her head, and instead she puts on a pirate patch and wields a gladiator sword.

"At a dinner party it's important that you stand out," says Marge, buttoning Jake into a yellow sequined jacket. "I was at a dinner party in Paris when I caught the eye of the earl of Toulouse, and he taught me to tango."

"What's tango?" Jake is squinting at Marge.

"I'll show you," says Marge, and she picks

my little brother up into a hug and dances him around the room, singing loudly.

"The earl of Toulouse taught me to dance like this, but he had a rose between his teeth and a red monkey jacket on." Marge looks giddy with the memory.

Jake and I catch each other's eyes as Marge warbles on, and I start laughing so much my chest hurts. Then I remember Mommy has a pink feather boa. It's really soft and silky, and she lets me wear it if I am very careful.

The boa would look perfect with Marge's hair, so I find the box and offer it to her.

"You should wear it," says Marge kindly.

I finally choose a sparkly evening gown and tall heels to go with the feather boa. I also wear Mommy's gold bracelets looped over my ears—Marge says I look like a baroness. Jake matches Dad's Wellington boots with his sequined jacket and a French beret, which is a kind of

French hat that makes adults look silly.

Marge grabs Dad's black tuxedo jacket and folds up the sleeves to fit her short arms. And she adds the suit pants, which are so long they touch the ground and she has to fold them up. She even finds his bow tie and a top hat. Then she grabs a black marker from her handbag and draws a twirly-whirly mustache on her face. "I'm Marge, the man," she announces in a gruff voice.

"Mustaches make gentlemen look mysterious!" she says, bowing.

Marge and I admire ourselves in Mommy's large mirror until we are distracted by the noise of Jakey jumping dangerously fast on Mommy's bed.

"That looks like fun!" says Marge, and she joins in. Soon we are all jumping on the bed, and I finally understand why Jakey does it all the time.

My legs are so tired they are wobbly, and my tummy is really rumbling when Marge holds out the list and sings, "It's time for the dinner party to start!"

"Who are the surprise special guests?" Jakey wants to know.

As we walk downstairs, I am struck by a brilliant idea. I sneak off and return with a shoe box that has holes poked in the top.

"Ta-da!" I cry.

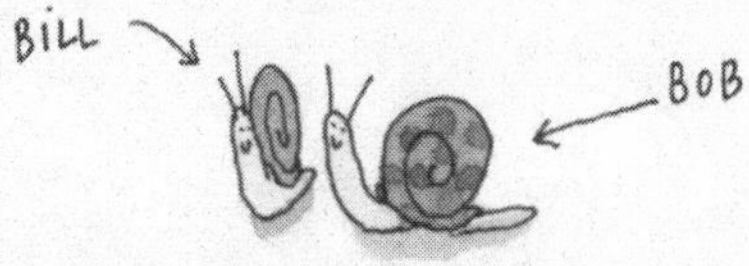

I lift the lid.

"Marge, meet Bill and Bob, our pet snails. They can be our special dinner guests!"

Marge looks pleased, and Jake whoops with excitement.

"Mommy says they have to stay in the box, but this is a special occasion and we need six guests," I reason, lifting them out gently and setting them on the table.

"They leave a shimmery trail behind them like gooey fairy dust!" Jakey adds.

"Now that we have our guests, we can start!" Marge says with a cheer.

Archie looks confused as Marge puts him in Jakey's old high chair. He is not normally even allowed to be in the dining room, and now he is sitting at the table with two chopsticks in front of his paws!

I feel like a princess in my sparkly gown. Jake takes everyone's orders very politely, gives his notepad to Marge, then sits quietly in his chair. I have never seen him so well behaved or with such clean hair. If only Mommy could see him now!

There are a lot of banging and crashing sounds from the kitchen before Marge brings out one large bowl covered by a silver lid.

I'm really hungry now, so I'm very excited.

"Chef Marge has your appetizer!"

Marge lifts the lid dramatically and, underneath, the bowl contains brown goo and six spoons.

"I am *not* eating *that*!" Jakey groans. He's looking a little bit grumpy—I think he might be hungry too.

"It's *Soup à la Chocolatay*," Marge announces in a perfect French accent.

"It's not the hair dye again, is it?" I ask, sniffing the bowl.

Our babysitter dips her spoon daintily into the "soup" before taking a big **SLURRRP** from her bowl.

"It's chocolate soup," she says proudly. "I melted three whole bars and five mini ones that I found in my handbag."

Chocolate soup?

Marge is my favorite babysitter ever! "Mommy never lets us eat chocolate unless it's a special treat," I explain.

"Marge is in charge," says Jake cheerfully as he spoons some chocolate soup into his mouth. I have never seen Jake eat anything with a spoon before—he normally uses his fingers.

The melted chocolate smells delicious, so I pick up a spoon and have a taste.

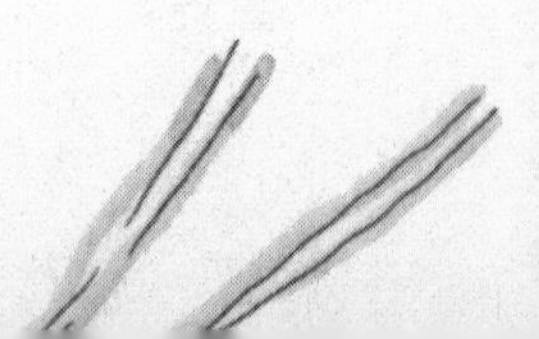

"Scrummy yummy in my tummy!" I say. That's what Grandpa Bert always says when he tastes anything delectable.

It's so tasty that before we know it, Marge, Jakey, and I are hugging the bowl between us and licking the inside and our fingers, and chocolate is everywhere and Marge's mustache is smeared with chocolate. Unfortunately there isn't enough left for the other guests at the dinner party.

Oops! I forgot about our special guests. Bill and Bob have inched away, but Archie looks disappointed.

Marge goes back to the kitchen to get the next course of the meal.

It feels like she is gone for a really long time, and we are REALLY hungry now.

Finally Marge returns. "And now for our main course!" she announces in her silly French accent. "*Voilà* macaroni and cheese."

Marge shows Jake and me which fork to use and how to look elegant while eating pasta. "Lady Beauregard always told me never to trust anyone who uses a spoon when they should use a fork."

Archie does not look elegant as he wolfs down his portion of pasta—there is cheese sauce all over his furry face. He licks it off.

SLURP! SLURP!

"And now for dessert," says Marge after we have finished. She disappears into the kitchen, and I share a look with Jakey. I hope we don't have to eat that cake we made!

But Marge has

a surprise in store. She returns with an enormous bowl of broccoli.

Jake shakes his head suspiciously. “That is NOT dessert. That is broccoli, and I refuse to eat it!”

“You are right, it is broccoli,” says Marge, smiling. “And we can’t eat broccoli at the dinner table,” she adds.

But eating our dinner was the first rule on Mommy’s list. What is Marge thinking?

“We can’t eat broccoli ANYWHERE,” says Jake crossly.

“What about on a bus?” Marge asks innocently. “Would you eat a broccoli tower on a bus?” Jakey’s eyes widen as Marge stacks all the broccoli stalks on top of each other until it’s a giant leaning tower of broccoli. Then she drags over the cardboard box that he uses as his superhero hideout. She takes chairs from the playroom and puts them in two rows in the box, just like the inside of a bus! Then she crawls inside the box and squeezes into the driver's seat!

"All aboard the bus, please," she calls.

Jakey mimes giving Marge his ticket, then races inside the box and takes a seat happily. I carefully bring over our broccoli tower and two bowls, and sit down too. Jakey and I each nibble a floret until the tower collapses, and then we pretend to wave out of the bus window.

Would you believe it? My brother eats all his broccoli! Mommy will be thrilled.

Not only has Jake eaten his broccoli, but he's used a fork, his hair is clean, and he can tango!

Marge looks happy too as she checks everything off the list and sighs.

"After a royal banquet or dinner party, the guests retire to the living room to chat," Marge explains, leading us out of the dining room. She proceeds to lie down across Dad's armchair.

Jakey and I snuggle up on the sofa. I don't even mind when Jakey leans his head on me.

"Don't you miss the palace?" I ask. I've never met anyone royal before.

"Never!" retorts Marge. "I left to travel the world seeking wild adventures in faraway lands!"

"Have you ever babysat before?" I ask.

"No, but I have petsat, plantsat, and housesat. I am usually very, incredibly, always, typically . . . busy," Marge replies with a yawn.

"What do you do for a job?" Jakey asks.

"Well, I try to take my puppies rollerskating every day, my ferret has an enormous hat collection and insists on trying on all the hats each morning, and my ponies like me to tell them stories while braiding their tails—and those are only half of my tasks," says Marge sleepily.

It's getting dark outside and I realize that it's probably past our bedtime, and our parents will soon be home. I think about the messy kitchen, Mommy's closet, and the bathroom full of bubbles. Marge notices my expression. She looks tired.

"The cleaner will be here shortly, I'm sure."

"Er, Marge . . ." I don't know how to break

it to her. "Marge—we don't have a cleaner!"

"What about a maid?" Marge asks, yawning.

I shake my head no.

"A butler?" Marge's eyelids are drooping.

Again, I shake my head.

"Not even a chambermaid?" she mumbles sleepily.

"No," I say. I don't even know what a chambermaid is!

But Marge has fallen asleep. Her skinny legs are thrown over the back of the chair and her belly rises and falls

with each snore.

I check the clock and it's five to eight. Uh-oh. We are going to be in *big* trouble. My stomach feels quivery.

"Jake, we only have five minutes till Mommy and Dad come back!" I whisper, so as not to wake our babysitter.

Jake jumps up in shock.

"We have to clean everything or Mommy and Dad won't let Marge come and look after us again!"

My little brother is looking at me with big, worried eyes. "Let's clean up, NOW!" he whispers back urgently.

I can't believe it, because Jakey HATES cleaning up! Whenever Mommy asks him to straighten anything, he just pushes it under the bed. He must really like our new babysitter.

We rush from room to room like little whirlwinds. The whole house is a disaster zone. There are towels and bubbles on the bathroom floor, Mommy's clothes are thrown around the living room, and the kitchen sink is piled up with chocolaty bowls. Marge is still fast asleep in Dad's armchair. Her messy rainbow hair is spread out, and she still has a black marker mustache and chocolate around her mouth.

Gently I wake her up. "Marge, it's time to clean your face and brush your hair before Mommy and Dad get back. We'll clean the house." She smiles sleepily at me and shuffles off toward the downstairs powder room.

Then I run around picking up Mommy's clothes while Jake grabs the mop and starts on the bathroom floor. I rinse the dishes and leave them in a sink full of hot, bubbly water. Jake puts Mommy's jewelry away, and I manage to make the dining room look normal again by tossing all our decorations into the laundry basket.

"Marge?" I call, wondering if she's finished getting ready. But she doesn't reply, and I can't see her anywhere downstairs—our babysitter has disappeared!

There's no time to find her—I can hear Mommy and Dad at the front door.

Quickly, we bolt upstairs to our bedroom and change into our pajamas. Archie is curled up sleeping on the rug in our room. Why isn't he sleeping in his own doggy bed? I scramble onto my top bunk and Jakey flings himself onto the bottom bunk just as Mommy creaks open our bedroom door.

I give a snorting sound that I hope Mommy will think is a snore.

Mommy and Dad kiss our faces softly as we pretend to be sleeping.

"They're fast asleep," Mommy whispers to Dad.

I hear them move toward the door.

"Is that Bob on the table?" she asks.

I open an eye. Oh no!

"Oh, and there's Bill," says Dad. "How did they get loose?"

Mommy picks up Bob and Bill and puts them into their shoe box before tiptoeing out of our bedroom.

The door closes quietly.

I wait a minute and then, leaving Jake snuggled in bed, sneak out onto the landing and peek through the bars of the staircase and down into the living room. To my surprise,

Marge is standing in the hallway, wide awake, with a clean face, and looking sensible, with all her magical hair hidden away!

I peer closer and see Archie's green blanket stuck to Marge's back like a cape.

That's why we couldn't find her—Marge must have crept off to sleep in Archie's doggy bed!

I snort back a giggle. I guess being small can be useful when it comes to finding comfy places to nap!

"How were they?" Dad asks.

"The kids ate all their dinner, even the broccoli, and Jake's hair is clean," Marge says proudly.

"Thank you!" Mommy says happily.

"It was easier washing my albino water buffalo's tail than Jake's hair, though," Marge says seriously, but Mommy and Dad laugh, thinking that she is making a joke.

Jake and I both know that she's not!

When I'm back in our room I wriggle under my covers and sigh in wonder.

"Are you awake, Jakey?" I ask.

"Almost," he says sleepily.

"Do you think Marge is a real duchess?" I ask.

Jake doesn't answer for a long time. Then I hear a giggle.

"Yes."

"Why are you laughing?" I ask.

"We have a royal babysitter," he says. "But *we* have to babysit *her*!"

Jake's right, and it makes me smile. "I hope that she comes again," I reply, snuggling into my pillow.

Jake and I are silent, thinking about it for a moment.

"Do you think Mommy would buy me some rainbow hair dye?" I ask. "Jakey, what do you think?"

But there is only the soft sound of his breathing.

"Night-night, Jakey," I whisper, and I turn out my light and drift off to sleep.

Marge at the Birthday Party

Hi! Remember me? I'm Jemima Button. I am seven years old and still the tallest in my class—though Rosie Williams is catching up with me now.

It's nine o'clock on Saturday morning. Jakey and I are downstairs eating eggs and toast. Jake is secretly feeding our puppy, Archie, all the runny yellow part of the egg, which he calls the "yuk" instead of the "yolk." I have finished mine, and now I'm drawing a picture of Granny's tabby cat, George, who looks like an old man with a yellow beard.

Today I have butterflies in my tummy because Marge, our amazing babysitter, is taking us to Theo's party. Theo is Jake's best friend from school. He has one long eyebrow and always shares his snacks with Jake. Even though I am very excited to see Marge, I won't know anyone at the party. I will be the oldest child there and possibly the only girl! What if no one plays with me?

Mommy and Dad can't come because they have to drive a long way today to visit Aunt Sally, who just had a baby. I'd love to meet baby Zara, but I get carsick.

"Are you two going to be on your best behavior for Marge today?" asks Dad.

Jake and I share a hidden smile and nod our heads.

But we can't promise that Marge will be on her best behavior! She always seems sensible until Mommy and Dad leave, and then we end up having fun and making up our own rules to add to Mommy's list. Marge is secretly a duchess who used to live in a huge royal palace. But she hung up her tiara to live a life of incredible adventures. And anyway, she couldn't fit all her extraordinary pets into the palace stables!

DING DONG—

Marge is here!

We jump up and run for the door. Jakey beats me there and pulls it open. Our babysitter smiles from the doorstep.

"Look, I had a splinter yesterday!" cries my little brother. He lifts up his foot for Marge to see the scratch on his heel. "Dad took it out with tweezers, and I didn't even cry," he brags.

"Very brave," says Marge, pinching his chubby cheeks. Jake never allows anyone else to do that!

Today Marge looks even smaller than I remembered. Can grown-ups shrink? She's wearing a colorful jacket, striped leggings, and a tall hat to hide her long rainbow hair.

"*Buon giorno!*" Marge smiles at me. "That is how Italian people say hello!"

Jake and I start to giggle.

"He-ll-o," Jakey replies in his robot voice. "*Buon gior-no. . . .*"

"The rules are on the fridge," Mommy tells Marge as she fishes in her purse for the car keys. Looking at us, she adds, "Remember to be polite and say 'please' and 'thank you' when Marge takes care of you."

Dad is heading toward the door. "Be good, you two. Enjoy the party."

"I won't know anyone there!" I gulp.

"Parties are a great opportunity to make friends," Dad says.

"Take a book to read," Mommy offers, trying to be helpful.

I imagine myself sitting reading, away from everyone else playing and having fun at the party. It makes me feel sad.

Mommy and Dad give both Jake and me big kisses.

We stand on the doorstep waving goodbye. As soon as the car disappears, Marge turns to me.

"Do you see this?" She shows me a tiny silver necklace with half a heart. I hold it in my fingers. There is small writing engraved on it. It reads: *Best Friends Forever*.

"This is a friendship necklace given to me by Chester."

"Who is Chester?" I ask.

Marge settles into Dad's brown armchair, and we come in close to listen to her story. Marge tells the best stories.

"I met Count Chester the meerkat at an amazing party. There were balloon elephants and fire jugglers, and I somehow got stuck in a giant bubble! Count Chester used his tiny claws to poke a Marge-sized hole in the bubble and set me free."

Jake and I are openmouthed.

"We became best friends for life!" Marge smiles. "You could make an extraordinary friend like Chester today too, Jemima." I think about it.

Marge slips off her jacket to reveal a black T-shirt with a lightning bolt across the middle and takes off her tall hat, and out tumbles her mass of rainbow-colored hair. Now she is really here!

"Let's read that list. Hop to it!" Marge twirls toward the fridge, her tiny shiny shoes tapping on the kitchen floor as she whirls. She reminds me of a colored spinning wheel.

"Today I can only read upside down," she announces, bending over as she reads:

1. Theo's present is in the top drawer —please wrap.

2. Party is at 11 o'clock at the park.

3. Only one slice of cake at the party.

Marge finds Mommy's fountain pen by the phone.

She crosses out "only one slice" and writes NINE slices.

"Yay!" yells Jake.

Marge is in charge!

"Let's not fill up on too much healthy food today. We need to leave plenty of room for cake!" Marge says, laughing. "Let's get started."

I show her the drawer with the present. It is a giant plastic water pistol!

"Ohh, let's open it now!" Marge suggests, and Jakey grins and claps his hands.

"I don't think we should," I warn them. "Theo won't want a birthday present that has been played with."

Oh no! Marge is already breaking the rules. I feel knots in my belly—I don't want to get into trouble with Mommy.

But Marge is holding the box and looking really excited. "At the palace we had an official toy tester whose job was to make sure all the toys worked before they were given as gifts! Today we can be the toy testers!"

"Fantastico," Jakey agrees. Jakey only says "Fantastico" whenever something amazing happens. Like the time he won a contest for eating the most strawberry shoelace candy.

I can't help but smile. Toy testers? I guess that makes sense. Marge has already succeeded in cheering me up.

Marge grins and adds a new rule to Mommy's list.

Have a water fight before the party.

We open the box and fill up the water pistol. But we don't fill it with water—we fill it with apple juice, because Marge says then we can take a sip if we get thirsty. Marge puts on her sunglasses.

"I don't want juice in my eyes," she explains. "I have very sensitive eyes. At the palace, I used to polish the emeralds and rubies on the queen's crown because my eyes were able to see even the tiniest speck of dust."

When the apple juice pistol is ready, I want to take a turn first because I am the oldest, but Jakey grabs it from me.

"Hey," I say, snatching it back. Then Jakey gets mad and pulls my hair!

OUCH. It really hurts. Mommy normally gives Jakey a time-out when he is naughty, but she isn't here, and my eyes begin to fill with tears.

"Jake!" Marge scolds, peering over the top of her sunglasses. "If anyone used their arms and legs to get their way at the palace, they were made to trim all the hedges in His Majesty's gardens with nail scissors!"

Jake looks surprised. "Nail scissors are tiny. And hedges are huge!"

"Exactly," says Marge. "Please apologize."

"I'm sorry, Jemima," my little brother says quietly. And would you believe that he gives me a hug? I ruffle his blond hair affectionately. I can't help it—no matter what my brother does, I love him so much.

Then we have the most amazing juice pistol fight. . . .

SPLISH! goes the juice on my dress!

SPLASH! goes the juice on Jake's sweater!

WOOF!
SPLOSH! goes the juice on Marge's fancy black shoes!

We end up wrestling on the carpet, and Archie starts chasing his tail and barking! I don't think I have ever laughed so hard in my life. Eventually Marge decides it's time to get ready, and we have to wash our hands and faces because of the apple juice.

Now, my little brother has two rules (in addition to no broccoli eating and no hair washing):

1. He won't wear a hat (even in the summer).

2. He never washes his face—EVER.

But would you believe it, when Marge asks him, he washes his face and even uses soap—**WOW!**

He looks very pleased with himself as well.

Back in the living room, Marge notices

the gold shiny wrapping paper for wrapping Theo's birthday present. "Ooh, that paper would make lovely party hats," she says. "Party hats are incredibly useful. All good parties end in a cake fight, and party hats will protect our hair!"

So we make hats, and as we cut and glue, Marge tells us the best story ever. It is about a spectacular cake fight that happened on her last birthday. At the end of the fight, she was covered in a twelve-tier pink sponge cake with chocolate mousse icing.

"There was cake wedged in butler Jones's reading glasses, and I had chocolate mousse up my nose and behind my ears for a week, and all because we didn't have hats!"

I most definitely do not want cake up my nose! I once got a frozen pea stuck up there, and Mommy made me blow my nose until it popped out. It really hurt.

Even though Mommy never lets Jakey use the grown-up scissors, Marge does, but she stands by his side the whole time. Jake cuts out three crowns from the shiny paper very carefully, with his tongue poked out in concentration.

We look like three glorious kings as we

parade around the whole house! I still can't believe that Jake has agreed to wear a hat. As we parade around, Marge sings us a song:

I dance around like a ballerina while Jake follows, banging a wooden spoon as loudly as he can on a frying pan. Marge tells us that the last time she was in a royal procession, she was nine years old.

"I secretly untied the grand duke's boot laces as he marched across the drawbridge."

Jakey thinks this is hilarious.

"Was the duke mad at you?" I ask.

"No! He had a lovely swim with the royal swans. Swans are very snuggly, you know, because of their long necks."

I try to picture cuddling a swan, and it makes me laugh again. I bet Marge was a very naughty child, like Jakey.

At last we come to a stop in the living room.

"What will we wrap Theo's water pistol in now?" I ask.

Marge closes her eyes and says in a serious voice:

"Hocus-pocus,
help me to focus!"

Then she reaches into her bag, and a long yellow silk scarf appears magically! She ties an enormous bow around Theo's present.

"Harry Houdini taught me how to tie a bow like that," Marge says.

"Who's Harry Houdini?" Jake and I ask in unison.

"The world's greatest magician. He could disappear and reappear from anywhere."

"Archie our puppy does that at the park!" says Jake.

We all look at Archie and decide that he must be a magical dog.

Marge tips her head upside down and consults Mommy's list again.

"It says to arrive at the party at eleven o'clock."

Jakey and I look up at the clock. The big hand is on the six and the little hand is on the ten. I count on my fingers.

"Marge, that's in half an hour," I say.

"No, that's in twenty hours," Jake corrects me. Marge and I exchange a look. Jakey hasn't learned to tell the time yet, but we don't want to embarrass him.

"Let's get dressed," says Marge. "All parties have a dress code. Usually something very bright and special for birthdays." She leads us upstairs to our bedroom, two steps at a time. Archie chases after us, and Marge explains that the dressing up includes him too!

Archie's furry head is cocked to one side. I think he can understand English, but no one except Jakey believes me.

"I don't think dogs are invited," I say.

Marge is riffling through my closet but pauses to protest. "Dogs love parties and birthday cake as much as people do, although you must always brush their fangs with mint toothpaste afterward."

So we decide on my green lace dress for Archie. It's too big, but I have to admit the color really suits him.

I put on my best dress. It's bright pink. Jakey lets me dress him in the blazer he got from Granny at Christmas.

After we are dressed, Marge tells us that no party is complete without a lot of balloons! Inside Marge's magical bag is a large bag with balloons in all kinds of colors as well as a small helium tank. So we sit in a circle taking turns blowing up as many balloons as we can. I choose the blue and red ones, and Jake does the yellow and green, and Marge blows up two at a time of any color she can find!

"Let's let them go," says Marge, watching hers float up to the ceiling.

The balloons get bigger and bigger, and we blow up more and more. Soon our living-room ceiling is hidden in rainbow bubbles. There are so many balloons I almost can't see Jakey or Marge!

"I once got my feet tangled in fifty balloons and floated all the way across the city," Marge declares, popping her head out between the balloons. "My hairdo was completely ruined in the wind, and everyone saw my underwear! It was embarrassing."

Jake grabs a purple balloon and sits on it like a whoopee cushion. **POP!**

We all giggle.

"Marge . . . ," I say, looking at the clock again, "I think it's time to go!" I hate being late.

We leave the house with Archie dragging his dress behind him and an enormous cloud of rainbow balloons all bobbing and bumping into each other above our heads. I start to feel nervous again.

I have brought my book with me, just in case I get bored or lonely.

Theo's party is under the big oak tree in the little park near our house. It has been decorated with streamers and a banner reading FIVE YEARS OLD TODAY! There is a tablecloth laid out over a wooden picnic table covered with cupcakes and sandwiches and a big pile of presents. Next to the tree is a giant bounce castle.

Now, if there is one thing Jakey and I really

love in the world, it is bounce castles. I wish my whole bedroom were a bounce castle and that the bottoms of my sneakers were made of bounce castles too!

All the little boys are very happy to see Jakey, and they say hi to us. I notice a few of them have their big siblings with them too. Josh's big sister, Posy, is here and Lucy Walker, Theo's sister, as well. I feel much, much better seeing other girls my age at the party. Everyone laughs when they see Archie in a dress, particularly Theo! Theo doesn't even mind when Archie manages to steal a peanut butter cupcake.

"Happy Birthday, Theo!"

Marge, Jakey, and I chorus as we hand over his present. Theo looks surprised by the yellow bow.

"Don't worry," Marge tells him, "we tested the water pistol out for you. It's ready to use and filled with apple juice!"

"Thanks!" says Theo, taking in Marge's height. "Are you a child or a grown-up?" he asks, which makes me giggle.

Jakey explains very politely that Marge is actually a small grown-up, but that she is tall enough to ride a bike without training wheels, which is the only thing that matters.

Just as we take off our shoes to go into the bounce castle, disaster strikes! The sky clouds over and it starts to rain. At first it's just the pitter-patter of little drops, but soon they turn into big, fat blobs of water. Theo looks like he might cry. I would be really disappointed too if it were my birthday.

Theo's mom explains that we can't go into the bounce castle when it's wet because it's too slippery and slidey. "We don't want anyone bumping heads," she says.

But Marge has the most brilliant idea. "Masterful Marge to the rescue!" she calls as she gathers all the balloons we brought with us. She ties them into a big bundle, so big

and thick it makes a roof for the bounce castle. No rain can get in at all!

All the parents clap and cheer. I feel so proud that we brought Marge to the party and that she is our babysitter.

"Everyone into the bounce castle," Theo's mom shouts, and we all scramble up excitedly. Even Archie scampers up with us. His furry ears flap as he gets bounced up and down.

What fun! Whenever I am in a bounce castle, I imagine what it would be like to be a bird and be able to fly. Jakey is jumping so high his pants keep slipping down!

After a while our legs are tired, and we sit down in the bounce castle looking for something else to do. But it's still raining, so we can't run around in the park yet. Theo's mom and dad are looking anxious—all the party plans are going wrong.

I am just about to ask everyone if they want me to read them a chapter from my book, but then Marge jumps into the bounce castle with another brilliant idea.

"By day I am Magnificent Marge, Babysitter of Jemima and Jakey Button. But by night I am . . . Magical Marge the Magician!"

What is Marge up to? I wonder. We all crowd around Marge to see.

"I need a drum roll," she says dramatically. Theo's big sister, Lucy, is standing next to me, and she claps her hands as loudly as she can.

I join in, and soon everyone is clapping.

Marge twirls around and loses her balance on the grooves of the bounce castle, her skinny legs buckling, but recovers quickly. Theo's little brother, Matthew, tries not to giggle.

Then Marge does a loud fake cough, covering her mouth with her hand, and when she pulls it away there is . . . a purple silk handkerchief!

"Abra-ca-zebra!" she cries, looking very pleased with herself. "Now, this looks like an ordinary handkerchief, but look again."

We peer closely at the purple handkerchief. There is nothing weird about it, but then . . .

Marge's nose begins to twitch, and she emits an enormous sneeze.

The birthday boy is unimpressed. Theo says, "You don't need to be a magician to sneeze!"

But Marge smiles mysteriously and blows into the handkerchief as if it were a balloon. Then she shakes the purple silk, and lo and behold, out fly twenty pink lollipops!

Everyone grabs one. Mine tastes like watermelon, which is my favorite flavor of lollipops, even though I don't like the actual fruit.

Then Marge enlists the help of Archie as her magician's assistant! For her second trick she pulls a peanut butter cupcake out of her hat and then eats it using no hands, with Archie helping by licking up the crumbs.

"How did you learn magic?" Theo's friend Jack wants to know.

"Are you ready for a long story?" Marge replies.

We sit happily in a circle around Marge. Lucy sits next to me, which is nice, and we share a shy smile.

"One day a magician called Eduardo Alberti appeared at the palace to do magic for the whole village. As he was preparing for his grand show, his assistant was trampled by a herd of pink flamingos. So he picked me and my twin sister, Midge, to be his assistants!"

Marge has a twin sister called Midge? I can't wait to meet her.

"What did you have to do?" asks Theo, his eyes as wide as saucers.

"Eduardo hid me in a box so you could only see my head and shoulders, and Midge in the other half of the box so you could only see her knees and legs—and then he sawed us in half!"

We all scream in unison.

"Show me how to do the tricks," begs Theo.

"As a member of the Magic Triangle," Marge says seriously, "I am sworn to secrecy."

Jakey and I can't believe it.

Marge has led the most incredible and amazing life of any grown-up we know!

Next she juggles three balloons—well, she starts juggling with five, but one floats away and another pops when Archie bites it.

"Now for my final trick," Marge says as she produces a deck of cards with a flourish. Suddenly she throws them in the air and sings:

"Cards, cards, fly up in the air.
Make the weather fine and fair.
On this magical birthday,
Send the rain far away!"

We all scamper all over the place catching the cards as they fall around us. I reach high to catch the ace of hearts.

"Look!" shouts Lucy.

We stare up at the sky. Would you believe that it has completely stopped raining?

I look at Jake's face. His eyes are bulging in disbelief. Is Marge a real magician?

We scramble out of the castle and back into our shoes. The boys all take off, stretching their legs and hollering with joy.

But now there seems to be another problem. Theo's father gets a phone call. When he switches off his phone, he does not look happy.

"The face painter's car has broken down in a big puddle. He can't come."

Marge doesn't need to be asked twice. "Luckily . . . ," she announces gallantly, "I was taught face painting by one of the princess's ladies-in-waiting, and I am actually very good."

She reaches into her bag and brings out some makeup and pens. We form a line around the bounce castle waiting for our turn.

I am a little hesitant to have Marge paint my face, as she once tried to use Mommy's hair dye as a face mask!

She puts white makeup and pink lipstick on Lucy's face. "You are Marie Antoinette, the French queen!" Then she paints my eyes with black eyeliner, which tickles at the beginning but then feels kind of

nice, and then paints my lips bright red. "You are Cleopatra!"

Marge transforms Theo, Jakey, Peter, Matthew, and Daniel into warlords and Vikings, and she puts cat whiskers on herself, Zach, and Stella; but Posy doesn't want her face painted, so she just watches.

Marge really has saved the day.

Lucy and I wander away from the party and take turns on the swing. I show her my red tongue from the watermelon lollipop and she shows me hers, and we giggle.

Can you believe that Lucy also has a little brother like me, she has also lost five teeth like me, and she also has a secret diary that not even her mommy knows about? We have so much in common!

It's time for the party games.

The first game is Pass the Present. My mommy always makes sure everyone gets a present when we play this game on my or Jakey's birthday. But Marge doesn't seem to know the rules. When the present reaches her, she just passes it from her left hand to her right hand until the music stops.

"I win!" She laughs, unwrapping a layer of paper.

"Marge!" I scold her. "You have to share the present!"

"Sorry!" says Marge guiltily. "When I lived in the palace, the king always let me win!" She hands the present along, and Theo's little brother, Matthew, finally wins!

After the games, Theo's mom calls out: "Everyone sit down, please!"

It's time to sing "Happy Birthday" to Theo and eat cake, so we find a place to sit cross-legged in front of the picnic bench.

"Happy birthday to you,
Happy birthday to you,"

we all sing. Jakey's voice is the loudest as he hugs his best friend.

Looking at Theo's big chocolate cake with five candles on it, I feel very hungry.

I sometimes wish, when I see a big cake like that, that I could stick my whole face into it and gobble it all up. But I remember to sit nicely as I lick my lips and wait patiently.

Just as the cake is placed in front of Theo and he draws in a big gulp of air to blow out the candles, Marge pops her head up and blows them out first!

Oh no! I think.

Silence. Everyone stops singing "Happy Birthday." No one has ever blown out the candles before except the birthday person. What bad manners!

Theo looks like he might be about to cry.

But suddenly the five candles relight, and we all gasp.

Candles relighting by themselves?

"What happened?" asks Theo. He looks confused.

"It's because YOU are a secret magician," Marge tells Theo.

"But I have never been a magician before," Theo says.

"I made the wish for you," Marge explains, "when I blew out the candles. That's my birthday present for you. Candle wishes always come true."

Theo gives a big puff and blows out the flames!

Whoopee!

Theo looks very happy, as though being a magician might be the best birthday present ever. Everyone claps and cheers, and all the grown-ups take photos with their phones.

"How did you do that, Marge?" I whisper.

"It's just a trick!" Marge winks. "A trick that I can't reveal unless you are a member of the Magic Square, which I am."

"I thought it's called the Magic Triangle?" corrects Josh.

"Possibly," concedes Marge.

Secretly I make a wish that Marge will always be our babysitter.

After this we all get absorbed in eating the food, and Marge says that the children are allowed nine slices of cake each; but after the sandwiches and chips and fruit salad and candy and nuts and popcorn, I am too full to eat more than three slices of birthday cake, and Jake only manages one (very big) one.

Marge reaches into her bag and pulls out her gold paper crown that we made earlier.

"So no one throws cake at me," she whispers to Lucy, and we laugh.

"I am going to nap before the cake fight starts." Marge yawns. "You know, Countess La Roo was able to marry off her two daughters by teaching them magic," our babysitter warbles as she curls up with Archie. And there she lies, her feet poking out from behind the bounce castle. Her gold crown is lopsided, and her face paint is smeared. But she is sound asleep. Lucy and I decide she looks adorable.

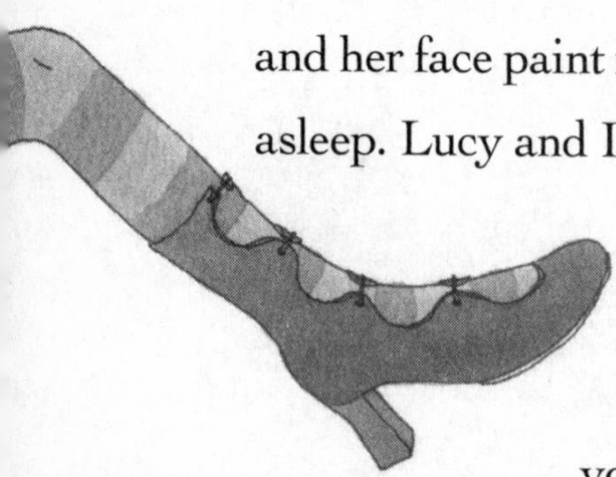

"Shh," says Lucy. "She needs her sleep after all that work. How old do you think Marge is?"

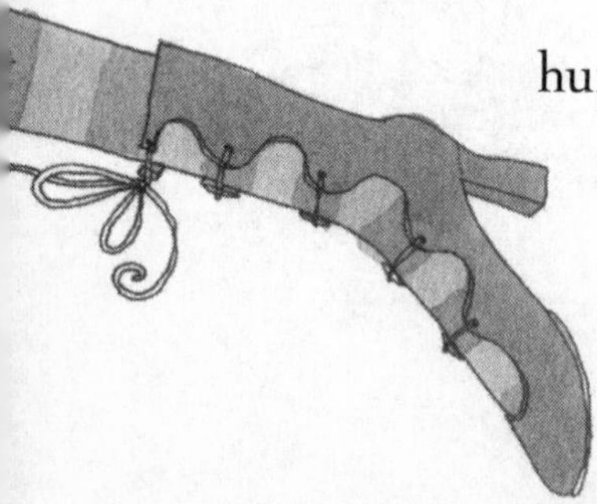

"Jake thinks that she is one hundred and fifty-one," I whisper, and we head over to where the other kids are playing.

I have a fantastic time playing with Theo, Jakey, and Lucy. We play Follow the Leader, with me and Lucy at the front and all the younger children following, until we arrive at the swings. Then Jake and Theo take turns pushing all of us back and forth.

HONK HONK!

I can hear Dad's horn!

I look over and see Mommy and Dad getting out of the car.

"*Buon giorno!*" I say as I run and give them a hug. They look exhausted from their long drive.

"How was the party?" asks Dad.

"I made a new friend called Lucy," I tell Mommy.

"That's great, Jemima! Well done," says Mommy.

"It was the best party ever!" says Jakey.

We all thank Theo and his parents for a wonderful time, and when Marge reappears with her face paint wiped off and looking very sensible, they thank her for saving the day.

"I can't believe that Jakey wore a hat!" Dad says when he hears about Jake's paper crown.

Then Mommy notices Archie.

"Is that your party dress, Jemima?" she asks me.

"Yes, Archie needed to be properly dressed to be a magician's assistant," Marge explains.

Mommy and Dad exchange a look.

"What a clever puppy, putting it on all by himself. Amazing paw control!" Dad jokes.

"He's the real Harry Houdini!" says Jake proudly, and we all laugh and laugh.

Marge at Large in School

Hi. Jemima Button here, with my little brother, Jakeypants. There are lots of things that Jake and I don't agree on. Jake prefers the shallow end of the pool and I like to swim in the deep end, and I always eat sweets slowly to make them last and he gobbles them up in one bite. But we both love to sit by the upstairs square window that looks down over our driveway. We call it the "spying window." Sometimes we spy on the neighbors walking their dog, and sometimes we count how many garbage cans there are on our street. But right now we are waiting for someone.

Marge, our royal babysitter and favorite

grown-up (after Mommy and Dad), is coming to take us to school today.

We are going to jump out and surprise her!

Even though it's seven o'clock on Monday morning and I have gym before lunch, I am still so excited because I love Marge. I love Marge as much as I hate gym (I'm the third-slowest runner in our class).

As Marge's mint-green Mini Cooper screeches into the driveway, my heart is racing.

"In position!" Jake shouts.

We run downstairs, and Jakeypants and I hide behind the front door. I have a sofa cushion as a weapon, and he has a pillow. Our puppy, Archie, is with us as well, and he keeps panting loudly.

"Shhh," I whisper at him, "or you'll have to hide somewhere else!

Marge can't know we're here." We wait, holding our breath. Her footsteps get closer.

DING DONG—that's the doorbell!

Jake and I squeeze farther back against the wall. The door handle turns.

Marge steps into the doorway. "Hellooooo," she calls to the empty hallway.

Jakey and I shout, "ATTACK!" and we both jump onto Marge.

I cling onto her back, and Jakey throws his pillow first and then grabs her leg. Archie barks and wags his tail in excitement.

"Argh!" screams Marge in surprise as she flies forward onto the carpet. I wrestle her, but she is so small and quick that she manages to roll away from us like a ninja.

"It's Marge the tickle monster," she calls, and begins tickling my stomach and Jakey's armpits. I throw a pillow at her head, but she ducks. We can't stop laughing, and Archie is yapping at us all tangled in a heap.

"Kids, get off Marge right now, please." Dad sounds mad as he passes through the hallway into his office.

Jakey and I spring to our feet as Mommy appears in the hallway.

"Sorry, Marge!" Mommy apologizes. She makes a stern "we'll talk about this later" face at us.

But Marge is smiling as Mommy helps her up. Marge is wearing a blue skirt with a beret.

"The list of things to remember is on the kitchen table," Mommy says, grabbing Dad's glasses for him, which he always forgets.

As Mommy gives Jake and me quick kisses good-bye, she says, "Remember to be polite and say 'please' and 'thank you' when Marge takes care of you. And no more wrestling the babysitter!"

"Have you seen my glasses?" Dad calls.

"I have them," Mommy answers as they both head out the door.

"Bye, kids. Have fun at school," our parents call as the door slams.

We three run upstairs and wave goodbye to them from the spying window. When their car is as small as an ant, Marge turns to us.

"*Bonjour,*" she sings as she pulls off her beret, and out tumbles her rainbow hair.

Holy hamburger!

It is plaited into a million tiny colored braids with little bows on the ends.

"*Bonjour* means *hello* in French. Now let's take a quick look at this list."

I fetch the list and bring Mommy's fountain pen too, as I know that Marge likes to add new rules of her own.

The list says:

1. Breakfast.
2. Pack school lunches.
3. Jakey must wear new school shoes.
4. Drop off at school at 8 o'clock.

"What's for breakfast?" Marge asks, swanning into the kitchen. "I'm feeling a little hungry—what are you both making me? Hop to it!"

Jakey looks at me with one eyebrow raised. I giggle.

"Marge, YOU are the grown-up! YOU are supposed to be making breakfast for us!" I explain.

"Oh!" Marge is surprised. "I've never made breakfast before. The queen's cook, Mabel, used to bring me breakfast in bed every morning," she says wistfully.

I am curious. "What did Mabel make you?"

"Royal Pancakes"—Marge sniffs—"with extra syrupy syrup."

"I love pancakes," Jake says. "I'm hungry!"

My tummy is grumbling too. What are we going to do about breakfast?

"I am sure that I can make you a pancake," Marge announces confidently. "How hard can it be? If Mabel can do it, so can Marge!" She takes Mommy's pen and adds Royal Pancakes to the first rule. "Marge's marvelous pancakes with extra syrupy syrup coming right up!"

Marge begins by rummaging around the kitchen in search of a pan and a bowl.

"You really don't have a butler or a chef to help me?" she asks after a while.

I giggle and shake my head. I wish we didn't have to go to school today. Spending time with Marge is so much fun!

I help Marge, and together we mix some eggs, butter, flour, and milk into a batter, and Jake whisks it up. Then Marge turns on the stove.

"Back away, little servants," Marge hollers as flames lick the giant pan. "I don't want to burn down the kingdom!"

Jake and I step away as Marge pours the entire mixture into the pan.

"I am actually making crepes, which is French for *pancakes*. They taste even more delicious!" Marge exclaims.

"Don't you want to use the spatula thing that flips the pancakes?" I squint at Marge. "That's what Mommy uses."

"Nonsense. Mabel the royal cook never needed to rely on fancy utensils. I am just going to toss it up in the air like . . . **THIS!**"

Marge grabs the pan with both hands and launches the pancake high in the air. Jake and I watch as it flies up, up, up and sticks SPLAT onto the ceiling!

"Call the guards, shut the drawbridge—we have a runaway pancake!" shouts Marge urgently.

I don't know what to think. The pancake is stuck on the ceiling, and it doesn't look like it's going anywhere.

"I think we should call the fire department," Jakey suggests. "They have a big ladder that we can climb to reach it."

"That's silly," I say. "The fire department can only come for emergencies."

"This is most definitely an emergency," Marge says gravely.

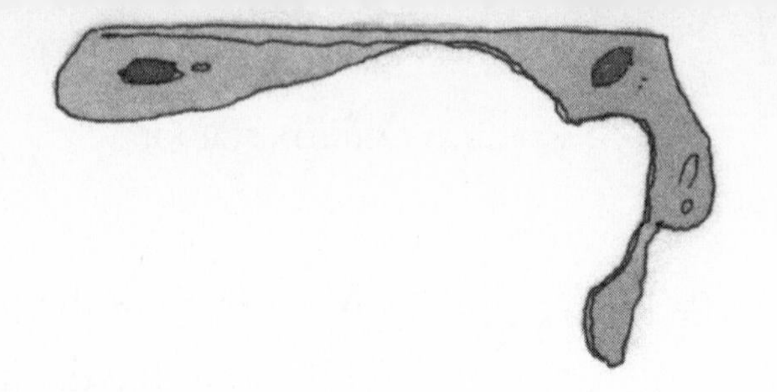

We all stare at the pancake for a few moments, thinking. Then Marge suggests we should just wait for it to drop back down into our mouths and catch it like Archie catches his ball.

But after we have waited with our mouths wide open for a while, my jaw is beginning to ache. "I'm so hungry and tired," complains Jake.

"Maybe it's still cooking," Marge offers hopefully.

"On the ceiling?" I ask.

Just when we are close to giving up and getting some cereal instead, gravity gets the better of the pancake.

PLOP!

Down it falls, landing right in the middle of Marge's head!

"Breakfast is served! Dig in," Marge says.

We grab forks and Marge pours syrup all over her head, and we eat it right off her hair in big, gooey gulps! Jake is so hungry, he ends up gobbling up half the pancake, so I have to stop him before he eats any of Marge's multi-colored hair!

"Here!" Jakey grabs Marge's beret. "I

think you need to put your hat back on—your hair looks very sticky!"

Marge reads Rule Two aloud in a French accent: "Pack school lunches."

I show her where Mommy keeps our lunch boxes in the fridge. She looks suspiciously at the sandwiches, sniffing the bread and cheese. In the end she decides that they are delicious and healthy but that we must have treats too. So she fills the rest of our lunch boxes with chocolate sprinkles from the baking drawer.

I grin, and Jake claps his hands. "Marge is in charge!" he declares.

Marge consults the list again. "Now for Rule Three: Jake, Mommy says you have to wear your new school shoes."

Jakey looks furious.

His little face has turned red like a traffic light. "I hate wearing shoes!" he yells.

"All shoes?" asks Marge.

"Yes," replies Jake. He looks determined.

So Marge runs out of the room and returns five minutes later with a big brown sack she has brought from the hallway closet.

"Ta-da," she says. "It's Super Marge to the rescue!"

She turns the sack upside down and pours out a mountain of shoes. There are hiking boots, roller skates, clown shoes, flippers, stilts, skis, and even a pair of ice skates.

"Do any of these look fun?" she asks my brother.

"I wanna wear the roller skates!" Jake says, grinning.

Marge laces them up.

"But I don't know how to roller-skate!" confesses Jake.

"Don't worry," Marge replies. "They can teach you at school!"

"Let's bring your school shoes too, just in case," I say sensibly, packing them in his backpack.

"From what I've heard, they can teach you everything at school," Marge says. "I would love to go myself one day."

"Didn't you have to go to school when you were a kid?" I ask Marge.

Marge pauses to think for a moment, then curls into Dad's armchair, which I am beginning to think of as Marge's story chair.

"Are you ready for a story?" Marge asks.

I love it when Marge tells us stories from her days at the palace. Marge gave up her life as a duchess because she hates rules. If you think living in a normal house has lots of rules, imagine living in a palace! But I don't want *too* long a story now, because we have to go to school soon, and I hate being late.

"Prince Rupert and I had a governess called Lady Morag. A governess is like a teacher for the royal family. She had pointy teeth, and she made us practice piano until our fingertips were sore."

PIANO CLASS:
With ~~Governess~~ Lady Morag
DRAGON

Oh no! Jakey and I share a look. She sounds terrifying. Poor Marge.

"One day Prince Rupert and I had had enough. We tricked Lady Morag into the dungeon and then locked her in with the rats and cobwebs."

Jake claps his hands with glee, but I think the palace dungeon sounds scary. Marge seems to understand.

"We let her out again, of course," she explains. "It wasn't for long, but she learned her lesson. Lady Morag was much nicer to all the royal children after that!"

Marge stands up, and we head to the door.

Suddenly Jakey's bottom lip starts to quiver, and he bursts into tears. "I don't want to go to school today!" he sniffs.

I know why my little brother is upset, so I tell Marge. "We are practicing for the school concert first, before class."

Jakey and I are obviously not in the same class, but we share music rehearsals with some of the other classes on Monday mornings. I like the practices, but Jake says they are lame. He does not enjoy playing the recorder.

"It's BORING," Jakey wails. "I'm allergic to music."

I give him a hug and try to cheer him up. "You just have to practice the notes."

Suddenly Marge springs to life and leaps onto the coffee table dramatically.

"By day I am Magnificent Marge the Babysitter, but by night I am Marge the Musician."

WOW! Marge is a musician too!

"I am the star of the Royal Brass Band," Marge boasts.

"What's a brass band?" asks Jakey, his tears drying up.

"It's a group of musicians who all play brass instruments like trumpets, horns, and the tuba," explains Marge.

"Who is in the band with you?" I ask, imagining her princess friends.

"No one," says Marge. "I play all the instruments by myself. I like to promenade in the royal gardens wearing all of them around my neck."

Jake seems to cheer up at this. "Will you come to our school concert rehearsal?"

"Of course!" says Marge, gathering our backpacks and putting her beret on.

Phew, we are finally setting off for school!

It turns out roller-skating is actually very hard! While Marge and I walk along the sidewalk chatting, Jakey's little legs pump faster and faster on the skates until we reach the top of a very big hill. After that he whizzes past us and disappears into some bushes! Extremely fast.

Marge and I look at each other, horrified. This reminds me of the time we lost Jakey at the supermarket when he was very small. He was finally discovered by Dad lying under the shopping cart, licking the wheels.

"Jakey?" I call, looking everywhere. I can't see him. My heart is starting to beat quicker. "How will I tell Mommy that we lost Jakey?" I worry.

"He's not lost," Marge explains. "He's temporarily missing."

We hear a scrabbling sound coming from the bushes. Then a brown squirrel darts out, followed by Jakey, who is covered in twigs and leaves. He grins from ear to ear. "I love skating, and I didn't even skin my knees!"

He's tired out, though, so I make him take the skates off and wear his school shoes. We are on our way to school again!

At the school gates, our music teacher, Mrs. Potts, is waiting to take everyone to music rehearsal. Marge introduces herself with an elaborate curtsy.

"How do you do? I was born Margery Beauregard Victoria Ponterfois, and I . . . am a duchess."

Mrs. Potts seems quite surprised when Marge insists on attending the rehearsal, because parents and friends aren't supposed to be in school. But after Marge points out that she is a musician herself in the Royal Brass Band, Mrs. Potts breaks the rules and allows her to come along.

I am slightly nervous about Marge being at school with us. What mischief will she create?

On the walk to the auditorium I overhear Marge confiding in Mrs. Potts, "I've never been to a school before. My last governess taught me needlepoint and wildflower pressing!"

"You were homeschooled?" asks Mrs. Potts.

"Palaceschooled," corrects Marge.

Mrs. Potts's mouth opens in surprise, and Jakey and I can't help but stifle giggles.

Everyone is staring at Marge as we enter the auditorium, as her beret is stuck on at a weird angle from all the syrup, and she is doing an excited little jig on the spot.

Mrs. Potts claps her hands twice for quiet, and Jakey and I sit down with Rosie, William, Lucy, and Theo. They all remember Marge from Theo's party and wave hello. Marge stands at the front of the auditorium with our music teacher.

"Good morning, girls and boys," says Mrs. Potts. She smiles brightly as we all say good morning back to her (except for Jakey, who is looking nervously at the musical instruments in the corner).

"Meet Jemima and Jake's babysitter, Margery Beauregard Victoria . . . *Porcupine*?"

Everyone laughs.

"Er, sorry if I got that wrong," says Mrs. Potts. "Anyway, Marge is going to help us today."

Marge takes a bow as if she is being given an award, then dances from foot to foot like the ground is boiling hot, which makes everyone laugh.

Mrs. Potts is looking flustered again.

"Oh no," she says, rummaging through her papers. She turns to Marge. "It appears I've left the sheet music behind. I'll be right back. Will you watch the children until I return?"

Marge nods enthusiastically.

Jake and I exchange a look. I can't believe

that Marge is in charge of an entire auditorium of children!

As soon as Mrs. Potts has left, Judy Briggs puts up her hand. "Are you a child or a grown-up?" she asks Marge. Everyone giggles again.

"Jake will explain," Marge replies.

So Jakey stands up and politely tells the whole class that Marge is actually a very small grown-up, but that she is tall enough to reach the middle shelf of the fridge—the cheese shelf—which is all that matters. Jakey loves cheese as much as I love sticker books. Everyone nods in agreement.

"Let's begin class," Marge announces in an important voice. "I am your temporary governess, so please line up while I hand out your musical instruments."

Marge has found the big blue bucket in the

corner filled with all the instruments and is standing by it proudly.

As we each make our way to Marge, I notice that some of the boys are taller than Marge, which makes me giggle.

Marge closes her eyes and fishes into the bucket.

There is a moment of silence before she says, "*Voilà!*" and pulls out a clarinet.

She hands it to Rosie Williams, who looks confused.

"But I play the violin," Rosie says as the rest of the class laughs.

Marge thinks for a minute. "Not today you don't. Everyone should learn how to play as many instruments as they want. How else will you find the ones you like the most? I myself have fourteen favorite instruments. I am as accomplished on the French horn as I

am on the Scottish bagpipes."

Marge fishes back in the bucket.

"Next!" she calls.

Judy is next in line and is given a guitar instead of her flute.

Then it's Jakey's turn. Marge fishes in the bucket, humming with her eyes closed, and pulls out a triangle.

"But I don't know how to play it!" Jakey worries. "And if I am not very good on the recorder, I will be terrible on the triangle."

"Nonsense," says Marge. "Just listen to your heart, and you will make wonderful music. NEXT!"

I am next in line, and Marge fishes out a trumpet. I love the sound that a trumpet makes, but I have never thought of playing it before. I usually play the violin, and no other girls in my grade play the trumpet. Suddenly

I feel quite excited to play a new instrument, and I put my mouth around the end and blow—**PFF!** A strange, raspy sound comes out.

One by one all the instruments get handed out until nearly everyone has an instrument that they have never played before. There is a small tug-of-war over the drums that is quickly resolved by Marge deciding that all three boys can play them at the same time.

A handful of the younger children haven't lined up for an instrument. "We don't want to play anything," Mary Cooper complains. "It's not fun."

"I'm going to make a special instrument just for you!" Marge says cheerfully.

Marge busies herself in the corner. She fills an empty jam jar with paper clips, pins, and staples, making a colorful shaker.

"Ohh . . ." Mary looks thrilled as she makes a rattle sound with it.

So we all help to make instruments for the children without them. I find an empty coffee can and make a drum. Judy manages to make a rainstick for Harrison's little brother. Marge finds some old bells, ties them to pieces of ribbon, and hands them out. Soon everyone is happy.

"Now we are ready for a concert!" cries Marge.

We're a little bit nervous, but gradually everyone starts playing.

"Close your eyes and make lots of noise! There is no wrong way to play music," Marge says as she sways in front of us.

We are all blowing, banging, strumming, dancing, clapping, and singing! The sound is so noisy that I can't hear my own trumpet even though it is very loud.

I look over at Jake. He looks so happy as he tings the shiny metal triangle in time to the music.

"You all sound excellent!" Marge says enthusiastically. "Let's share our wonderful music with the rest of the school!"

Marge flings open the door and leads the entire classroom through the hall and out onto the playground.

Even though it sounds terrible, we are all having tons of fun. I now understand why music makes you feel happy, even though I can't make anything but a raspberry sound come out of this trumpet. Rosie is playing her clarinet like it's a guitar, and Lucy is wearing a drum on her head.

"It's my drum hat," she says, and bangs it. It makes the funniest sound!

Theo is playing the violin backward! But you won't believe this—he's actually making a good noise. Jake is tinging his triangle proudly, and Marge is singing like she is in an opera! Her voice is shaky and shrill like a goat on a mountaintop.

We end up in the center of the playground, and we are making such a racket that all the other kids and teachers come out of their rooms and form an audience.

At first no one knows what to make of us, but soon the other kids start tapping their feet and clapping along. The teachers find it impossible to disapprove as we are clearly having so much fun. Even Mrs. Turnball, our strict science teacher, is nodding her head in

time with the music, and some of the older kids are dancing!

My cheeks are hurting from blowing and laughing, and everyone seems to love our crazy show!

But I can't see Marge anywhere. Where is she?

Then I hear a deep sound and turn around. Marge is wearing Jakey's roller skates and has strapped a tuba to her neck. The tuba is like a trumpet for a giant, and it is twice the size of her body! I have only seen an older girl called Martha play it before.

Marge is blowing the tuba loudly and skating around us all.

Oh no, Marge, you have gone too far, I think. She is twirling way too fast as she sails past me.

Mr Lindon, our gym teacher, shouts, "Watch out!" as Marge whizzes past him. But he is too late.

CRASH!

BANG!

SPLASH!

Marge has lost her balance and fallen into the little water fountain in the middle of the playground.

We all can't stop giggling as Mrs. Potts

arrives to see Marge in the fountain with her head stuck inside the tuba and just her little legs poking out!

Everyone is laughing their heads off, but Jakey and I rush forward and help Marge out of the water. Jake and Theo take hold of the tuba, and I grab her little feet and try to pull her out of it. Then Rosie takes a hold of me

and helps pull, and Lucy takes a hold of Rosie, and Jamie and Peter take a hold of Lucy, and before I know it all the kids have lined up and are pulling like a tug-of-war to get Marge free from the tuba. Until . . .

Marge is free! We all fall down, but no one is hurt and I'm relieved that Marge is okay, even if the tuba is a little wet.

"Well done, my fellow musicians!" Marge praises us, and we end up in a big group hug.

Just then Mr. Siles, our principal, appears on the playground. "All right, everyone, back to class," he says sternly. He raises an eyebrow at the sight of Marge, soaking wet, in a beret, holding a tuba.

"Marge, it's time for lessons now," I explain.

"Can I join your class?" she replies, running ahead to the classroom.

We all head back inside, and the morning passes quickly. I can tell that everyone is in a good mood after our concert in the playground. Even Mrs. Potts doesn't seem to mind about the tuba, and in math Mr. Bates gives us prizes for getting our answers right! I get the Star of the Day certificate, and Marge wins three gold stickers.

At recess Marge gives Jake, Theo, Jamie, and Peter roller-skating lessons in the playground. Then in gym Marge convinces Mr. Lindon that all throwing and catching should be done to music. It turns out that I never miss the ball when I am listening to Marge singing loudly, and for once I really enjoy gym!

In art Marge suggests that we finish our self-portraits blindfolded. I thought our art teacher, Mr. Brock, was going to lose his temper when Ella painted on Drew's sweater by accident and James knocked over an entire pot of green paint . . . but by the end of class, even Mr. Brock agrees that everyone's portraits look more unusual and that the exercise has "unlocked our creativity." It's so much fun having Marge at school!

RING! Now it's time for lunch.

We tidy up the art room and fetch our lunch boxes, ready to sit in our lunch circle. As I'm walking back to our classroom, Jakey pops up beside me. "Mrs. Potts said that I can join your class for lunch today because I was so well behaved in music rehearsal."

I can tell that Jakey is excited to see our babysitter again, and when we walk through the door, we see that Marge is sitting in the middle of the floor. Jakey runs to give her a hug. Our homeroom teacher, Mr. Gale, looks a little surprised, but I don't think he minds.

"Could you look after the children while I eat my lunch in the staff room?" he asks Marge.

"Of course!" Marge agrees, giving Jakey a big smile.

As we sit down in a circle around her, Marge brings out a lunch box and a giant spoon from her handbag.

"In the palace we had an official food tester whose job was to make sure that no one poisoned the king or queen!" She grins hopefully at us.

Everyone is happy to share a bite of their lunch with Marge.

One spoonful of Jack's jam sandwich . . . **YUM!**

Two spoonfuls of Sarah's pasta . . . **TOO COLD!**

Half of Rosie's peanut butter and apple . . . **TASTY!**

ALL of Eli's fish sticks . . . **DELISH!**

Marge rubs her belly and sighs. "In the palace after lunch we always had nap time. A duchess can get very tired, you know."

Marge stretches and snuggles into the beanbag in our library corner, next to her tuba.

"Will you read me a book?" she asks in a baby voice.

Lucy and I run and get our favorite storybook, and Eli gets a blanket from the cabinet. When Marge is tucked in, we read her a bedtime story. Jakey is in charge of turning the pages, and everyone joins in. We pass the book around the class and take turns reading a page each.

Once we have finished the story, Marge's eyes are closing.

"Can you leave the light on?" Marge asks. "I'm scared of ghosts."

Jakey rolls his eyes. "There is no such thing as ghosts! Even I know that, and I'm only four." He really is excellent at eye rolling.

"Yes, there are too ghosts," Marge replies. She pulls her blanket off and covers her head with it.

"WHOOOO!" she calls in a ghostly voice.

"WHOOO . . ."

Everyone in the class starts to giggle. Marge is so funny.

"It's me, Marge the Magnificent Ghost!"

Then Marge yawns sleepily, cuddles up to the tuba, and promptly dozes off.

When he gets back from lunch, Mr. Gale is very impressed at how quietly we're sitting in our lunch circle. He doesn't seem to notice that Marge is asleep in the corner and we are only being quiet because we don't want to wake her up.

I can't stop thinking about Marge for the rest of the day. I go from class to class wondering if Marge is still asleep or if she is up to any more mischief. I wish I could peek in on her and see if she is still asleep on the beanbag, but I don't have time, and the day seems to whizz past.

RING!

That's the bell telling me that school is finished for the day!

At the school gates I find Mommy, Dad, and Jakey waiting for me.

"How was school, Jemima?" Dad asks.

"I played the trumpet today!" I brag. "And I didn't miss the ball once during playing catch in gym."

"How were music rehearsals for you, Jakey?" Mommy asks my little brother. She looks a little worried, because he usually complains all the way home from school on Mondays.

"I LOVED music rehearsals," Jakey says happily. "Marge taught me to play the triangle, and Mrs. Potts said that because I like it so much, I can play it again next week!"

"Marge was in school?" Mommy asks, surprised.

At that moment I hear a familiar sound, and we all turn to look.

Marge is walking out of the school with the big, shiny tuba, playing a very loud tune. She pauses a moment and gives us a big smile.

"I blew all the water out of it!" Marge announces. "Mrs. Potts says that I can join the school band too. I just need to practice a bit at home first," she says excitedly.

Mommy and Dad share a look as Jakey and I crack up laughing.

"Where's my horse and carriage to take us home?" Marge asks.

"Very funny, Marge," Dad replies, pointing to our old blue car. Then he flings open the back door, bows down very low, and cries, "Your carriage awaits, Your Royal Highness!"

I'm giggling because Marge seems to bring out the funny side in everyone.

"*Merci!*" replies Marge in a posh voice. "That is French for *thank you*," she explains as we all bundle inside.

I can't help smiling all the way home as Jake